TANK WARFARE

Antony Loveless

Crabtree Publishing Company
www.crabtreebooks.com

Crabtree Publishing Company
www.crabtreebooks.com   1-800-387-7650
Copyright © **2009 CRABTREE PUBLISHING COMPANY**.
All rights reserved. No part of this publication may be reproduced, stored in a retrieval system or be transmitted in any form or by any means, electronic, mechanical, photocopying, recording, or otherwise, without the prior written permission of Crabtree Publishing Company.

**Published
in Canada
Crabtree Publishing**
616 Welland Ave.
St. Catharines, ON
L2M 5V6

**Published in the
United States
Crabtree Publishing**
PMB16A
350 Fifth Ave., Suite 3308
New York, NY 10118

Content development by Shakespeare Squared
www.ShakespeareSquared.com
First published in Great Britain in 2008 by ticktock Media Ltd,
2 Orchard Business Centre, North Farm Road,
Tunbridge Wells, Kent, TN2 3XF
Copyright © ticktock Entertainment Ltd 2008

Author: Antony Loveless
Project editor: Ruth Owen
Project designer: Sara Greasley
Photo research: Lizzie Knowles
Proofreader: Crystal Sikkens
Production coordinator:
  Katherine Kantor
Prepress technician:
  Katherine Kantor

With thanks to series editors Honor Head and Jean Coppendale.

Thank you to Lorraine Petersen and the members of nasen

Picture credits:
Alamy: Jack Sullivan: cover, p. 21, 24–25, 26
© Crown Copyright/MOD, image from www.photos.mod.uk. Reproduced with the permission of the Controller of Her Majesty's Stationery Office: Army: p. 28; Sergeant Paul Brownbridge: p. 14–15; Richard Ellis: p. 29; Sergeant B. Gamble: p. 20; WO2 Giles Penfound: p. 8–9
Corbis: Thaier Al-Sudani/Reuters: p. 12–13; Annie Griffiths Belt: p. 31; Kim Komenich/San Francisco Chronicle: p. 18–19; Leif Skoogfors: p. 14 (top); Shamil Zhumatov/Reuters: p. 13 (top)
Corbis Sygma: Jacques Langevin: p. 19 (top)
Getty Images: p. 16–17; AFP: p. 15 (top), 22–23, 31;
  Hulton Archive: p. 7; Time & Life Pictures: p. 6, 10–11
Rex Features: p. 4–5; Sabah Arar: p. 27
Shutterstock: p. 1
Superstock: Stocktrek: p. 2–3

Every effort has been made to trace copyright holders, and we apologize in advance for any omissions. We would be pleased to insert the appropriate acknowledgments in any subsequent edition of this publication.

Library and Archives Canada Cataloguing in Publication

Loveless, Antony
    Tank warfare / Antony Loveless.

(Crabtree contact)
Includes index.
ISBN 978-0-7787-3816-9 (bound).--ISBN 978-0-7787-3838-1 (pbk.)

1. Tanks (Military science)--Juvenile literature. 2. Tank warfare--Juvenile literature. I. Title. II. Series.

UG446.5.L69 2008   j358'.184   C2008-905955-7

Library of Congress Cataloging-in-Publication Data

Loveless, Antony.
    Tank warfare / Antony Loveless.
        p. cm. -- (Crabtree contact)
Includes index.
ISBN-13: 978-0-7787-3838-1 (pbk. : alk. paper)
ISBN-10: 0-7787-3838-8 (pbk. : alk. paper)
ISBN-13: 978-0-7787-3816-9 (library binding : alk. paper)
ISBN-10: 0-7787-3816-7 (library binding : alk. paper)
 1. Tanks (Military science)--Juvenile literature. 2. Tank warfare--Juvenile literature. I. Title.
    UG446.5.L59 2008
    358'.184--dc22
                                                2008039396

Contents

Chapter 1
What is Tank Warfare? 4

Chapter 2
The History of the Tank 6

Chapter 3
Tanks of Today 8

Chapter 4
Tank Crew 12

Chapter 5
Tanks at Work 20

Chapter 6
Stopping a Tank 24

Chapter 7
Tanks of the Future 28

Need-to-Know Words 30

Tough Tanks/ Tanks Online 31

Index 32

CHAPTER 1
WHAT IS TANK WARFARE

Tank warfare happens when an army uses **armored** fighting vehicles against an enemy. Tanks attack the enemy head-on.

Machine guns can turn to face the enemy.

Turret

Wheel

4

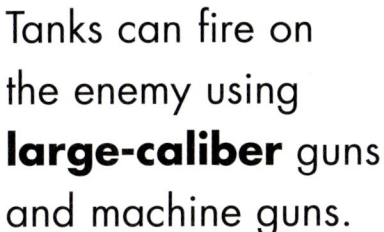

Tanks can fire on the enemy using **large-caliber** guns and machine guns.

Heavy armor and good **mobility** give the tank protection.

Large-caliber gun

Heavily armored **hull**

Tough tracks which do not puncture or tear like tires

Wide, thick tracks help the tank move fast across rough ground. The tracks spread out the tank's weight. This means the tank is less likely to get stuck in soft ground, mud, or snow.

CHAPTER 2
THE HISTORY OF THE TANK

During World War I, the military used trench warfare. This meant soldiers hid in **trenches**.

They had to climb out of the trenches and run across open land to attack the enemy. This was called "going over the top."

When it rained, soldiers slipped and fell in thick mud. They were easy targets as they ran in the open toward the enemy.

Soldiers "going over the top"

Trench

The British Army wanted a new way to capture enemy territory. They realized they needed a vehicle which could move over rough ground, fire at the enemy, and protect the soldiers inside.

British Mark A Whippet tank in 1918

The tank was developed very quickly. In less than three years, the tank rolled onto the World War I battlefields. The invention of the tank helped to end the war.

CHAPTER 3
TANKS OF TODAY

THE CHALLENGER 2

The FV4034 Challenger 2 is the British Army's main battle tank. It is very heavily armored.

The British Army has around 400 Challenger 2 tanks. Only three have ever been damaged in **combat**.

Here, a Challenger tank rolls off a transport ship in Kuwait. The tank is being transported to Iraq.

Cover to protect the gun in transit

Fuel drum

Rear of tank

FV4034 Challenger 2	
Cost	Over ten million dollars each
Top speed	Up to 40 mph (64 km/h)
Weight	68 tons (62 metric tons)
Crew	4 crew members

Transport ship

THE M1 ABRAMS TANK

The M1 Abrams is the U.S. Army's main tank.

The Abrams is nicknamed "Whispering Death" because its engines make little noise. The enemy cannot hear it coming!

The top panels of the tank blow outward if it is hit by a HEAT (High Explosive Anti-Tank) missile. This stops pieces of the damaged tank from hurting the crew inside.

An Abrams tank on a training exercise

M1 Abrams	
Cost	Nearly 4 million dollars each
Top speed	Up to 46 mph (74 km/h)
Weight	77 tons (70 metric tons)
Crew	4 crew members

Engine

Top panels

Armor

CHAPTER 4

TANK CREW

A tank crew has four members—a commander, an operator, a driver, and a gunner. The commander, operator, and gunner work in the turret.

The commander is in charge and reports back to headquarters. The commander makes sure the tank and its crew are working well.

A tank commander checking a machine gun

A tank operator loads rounds onto the tank.

The operator works the radio and loads rounds of **ammunition** into the guns. He also cooks for the crew.

Each member of the crew has his own job to do. However, the men are trained to do each other's jobs, too. This is important in case a crew member is ill or injured.

The tank driver sits in the front of the hull under the main gun.

To fit in the small space, he leans back in a seat that is like a dentist's chair.

Driver

The gunner controls the direction and angle of the turret and main gun.

The gunner pinpoints targets using a **sight** and a **laser range finder**. The laser measures the distance to a target.

Gunner

The driver steers the tank using a motorbike-style handlebar. The handlebar has a part called a throttle. The driver twists the throttle to make the tank move faster. The brake pedal is on the floor.

The driver keeps watch through the tank's three **periscopes**.

15

At night, the crew uses thermal night-vision equipment to see outside the tank.

Thermal-night vision equipment allows soldiers to see enemy tanks or soldiers without using normal lights.

There is not much room inside a tank. Four men share a space just 15 feet (4.5 meters) by 10 feet (3 meters), and about 6.5 feet (2 meters) high!

If the tank is in a desert, it can get very hot inside during the day. At night, it can be freezing cold.

When on duty, a tank crew lives, sleeps, and works in the same clothes for days.

There's no place to wash in the tank and it's often too dangerous to wash outside. The smell of soap can carry on the wind and reveal the soldiers' **position** to the enemy.

The toilet is a hole in the ground dug out with a shovel.

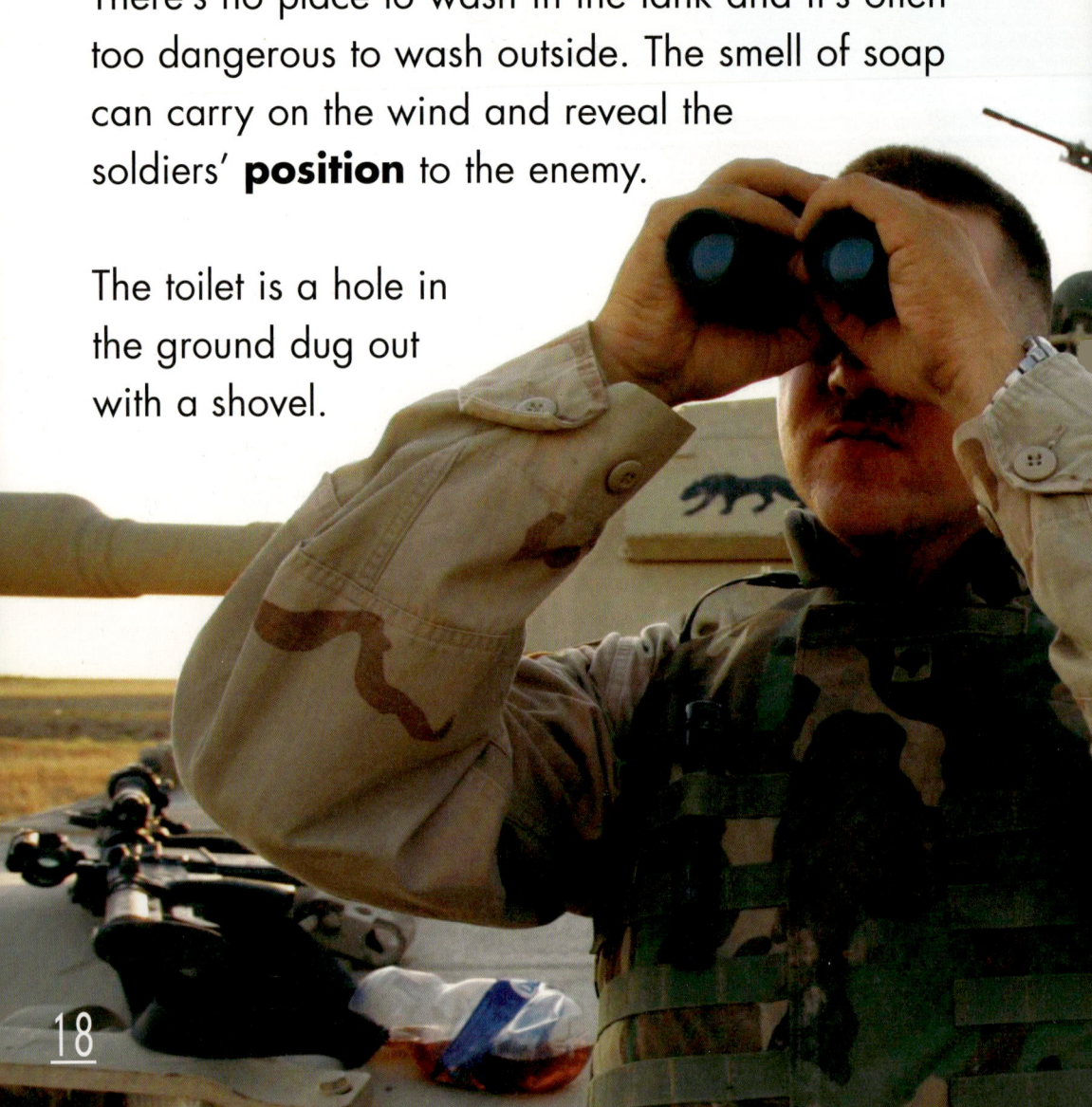

When on duty, the crew eats MRE (Meals, Ready-to-Eat) **rations**. These dry, **vacuum-packed** meals are often plain and tasteless.

Thankfully, the crews get chocolate bars and sweets in their rations.

Taking a break, but keeping watch for the enemy

CHAPTER 5

TANKS AT WORK

Tanks hardly ever work alone.
Normally, they work in a **platoon** of five.

Two tanks might **advance** while the other three tanks protect them from behind.

Tank platoon

Then the two tanks in front stop. The three tanks at the back then advance while the front two protect them.

A tank's turret can turn a full circle—360 degrees. The tank can shoot backward while moving forward.

Turret

Each tank in a platoon can have guns pointing in different directions.

This gives the platoon protection from all sides. The tanks can advance without stopping or slowing down.

When defending territory, tanks stay in a prepared position. This helps to protect the tank.

This tank is covered in leaves and green nets as *camouflage*.

A prepared position can be a hole or behind a hill. Only the tank's turret is visible. The crew can fire on the enemy, but most of their own tank is protected.

Sometimes tanks use trees as camouflage.

Tank commanders use IVIS (Inter-Vehicle Information System) to keep in touch with other tanks.

Tank commanders also send maps and share information about the enemy with other tanks. They use **radio** signals that are in code so enemies cannot understand them.

CHAPTER 6

STOPPING A TANK

Challenger 2 is one of the most heavily armored tanks in the world.

While on duty in Iraq, a Challenger came under attack. The enemy used machine guns and RPGs (Rocket-Propelled Grenades) to attack the tank.

The tank tried to reverse, but it fell into a ditch. The tank's tracks came off!

The Challenger was trapped.

The tank was hit by an **anti-tank missile**. Then it was hit by eight RPGs at close range. It was under attack for hours. But all the crew survived!

The crew stayed safely in the tank until they were rescued.

The tank's tracks were repaired and it was back to work six hours later.

The easiest way to stop a tank is to damage the tracks. Once these are damaged, the tank cannot move. This is called a "mobility kill."

The tracks and wheels of a tank are outside the armored hull.

When a tank goes over a hill, the enemy can fire at its underside.

The armor on the underside of a tank is not as thick as on the hull.

Enemies can fire on a tank from the tops of tall buildings.

The turret on a tank has to be light so that it can turn quickly. To make it lighter, the turret is not as heavily armored as the hull.

CHAPTER 7

TANKS OF THE FUTURE

In modern warfare, smaller, faster armored vehicles are often more useful to armies than the main battle tanks.

So, a new range of light armored tanks have been built.

A Scimitar crosses a floating bridge

Scimitars and Spartans are small tanks that can reach speeds of 50 mph (80 km/h). They can get close to an enemy and report back to headquarters about enemy positions and numbers. These smaller tanks are harder to spot than the larger Challengers and Abrams.

However, if they are spotted, they have the firepower to fight back!

Spartan tanks being transported by Chinook helicopters

NEED-TO-KNOW WORDS

advance To move forward

ammunition The objects fired from guns, such as bullets

anti-tank missile Powerful missiles made to destroy armored vehicles

armored Something that has a protective covering of metal

camouflage Something, such as leaves or a color, which helps a tank blend in to its background

combat Another word for fighting

hull The frame or body of a tank

large-caliber Describing the large measurement of the diameter of a gun's barrel

laser range finder A piece of equipment that uses a laser to work out the distance of an enemy object

mobility The ability to move easily

periscope A piece of equipment that allows a soldier to see outside the tank while he stays hidden inside

platoon A group of tanks or soldiers

position The place where an army or group of soldiers are hiding or waiting to attack

radio A piece of equipment that allows soldiers in one tank to talk to other tanks and to their headquarters

rations The food given to soldiers

sight A piece of equipment that a person looks through when they are aiming a gun or missile at a target

territory An area of land that belongs to a country or that has been captured by an army

trench A long, narrow ditch or hole dug in the ground

turret The top section of a tank where the guns are mounted. The turret can turn in a full circle to point the guns in any direction

vacuum-packed A way of packaging food so there is no air around it. This stops the food from going bad

TOUGH TANKS

What it takes for a tough tank

When designing a tank, the military considers three factors:
1. firepower
2. protection
3. mobility

These three factors must be in balance. For example, increasing a tank's protection by adding armor will increase the tank's weight. A heavy tank cannot move as well as a lighter tank. Increasing a tank's firepower by adding larger guns will also increase the tank's weight and limit how quickly the tank moves.

The M1 Abrams was invented in 1980. The design has since changed to improve its protection and mobility.

TANKS ONLINE

http://science.howstuffworks.com/m1-tank2.htm
Information about the M1 tank

www.tankmuseum.org/Vehicles
An on-line tank museum with photos and facts

www.generalpatton.org/education/interactive.asp
Click on the "Simple Machines" link to learn how tanks are built

Publisher's note to educators and parents:
Our editors have carefully reviewed these websites to ensure that they are suitable for children. Many websites change frequently, however, and we cannot guarantee that a site's future contents will continue to meet our high standards of quality and educational value. Be advised that children should be closely supervised whenever they access the Internet.

INDEX

A
Abrams (M1) tanks 10–11
armor 4–5, 8, 11, 24, 26–27

B
British Army 7, 8

C
camouflage 22–23
Challenger 2 (FV4034) tanks 8–9, 24
commanders 12, 23
cost (of tanks) 9, 11
crews 9, 11, 12–13, 18–19, 24

D
drivers 12, 14

G
guns 4–5, 8, 12–13, 14–15, 21, 24
gunners 12, 15

H
history of the tank 6–7

I
IVISs (Inter-Vehicle Information Systems) 23
invention of the tank 7

L
laser range finders 15

M
mobility (of tanks) 5, 26
MRE (Meals, Ready-to-Eat) 19

O
operators 12–13

P
periscopes 15
prepared positions 22–23

S
Scimitars 28
soldiers (protection of) 7, 24
Spartans 28–29
speed (of tanks) 9, 11, 28

T
tank life 18–19
tank platoons 20–21
tank warfare 4
tanks 4–5, 7, 8–9, 18, 20–21, 26–27, 28–29
thermal night-vision 16, 17
tracks 5, 24, 26
trench warfare 6–7
turrets 4, 12, 15, 21, 23, 27

U
U.S. Army 10

W
weight (of tanks) 9, 11
Whippet tanks 7
World War I 6-7